Under the Breadfruit Tree

Island Poems

by Monica Gunning

Illustrated by Fabricio Vanden Broeck

Wordsong
Boyds Mills Press

Published by Wordsong
Boyds Mills Press, Inc.
A Highlights Company
815 Church Street
Honesdale, Pennsylvania 18431
Printed in Mexico

Publisher Cataloging-in-Publication Data

Gunning, Monica.
  Under the breadfruit tree : island poems / by Monica Gunning ; illustrated
by Fabricio Vanden Broeck—1st.ed.
[48]p.: ill.; cm.
Summary: An original collection of poetry composed of a series of portraits from the poet's
childhood in Jamaica.
ISBN 1-56397-539-4
1. Children's poetry, Caribbean (English)—Juvenile poetry.
2. Caribbean area—Juvenile poetry. [1. Caribbean poetry
(English). 2. Caribbean Area—Poetry.] I. Vanden Broeck,
Fabricio, ill. II. Title.
811.220—dc21 1998 AC CIP
Library of Congress Catalog Card Number 91-91408

Book designed by Tim Gillner
The text of this book is set in 15-point Goudy.
The illustrations are scratchboard.

10 9 8 7 6 5 4 3 2

Contents

To my sons, Michael and Mark

—M. G.

For Nadia, Carlo, and Fabio
with love

—F. V. B.

Introduction

To help my friends who may not be familiar with Caribbean culture, I have provided a glossary below for words from the poems of *Under the Breadfruit Tree* that may be unfamiliar.

breadfruit—the edible fruit of the breadfruit tree, with a texture like bread when baked or roasted.

shilling—a coin used when Jamaica was a British colony

callaloo—a green vegetable with a spinachlike taste

congo peas—small, round green or brown beans

guavas—fruit with a greenish yellow rind and pink flesh

sorrel—a plant with acidic leaves that is boiled to make a delicious drink

bankra basket—a wide, flat-bottomed basket carried on top of the head

jipijapa hat—a Panama hat made with the fanlike leaves of the jipijapa plant

ackee—a delicate fruit eaten boiled, fried, steamed, or curried. Ackee and codfish is the national dish of Jamaica.

bulla cake—a flat cake without yeast or leavening

cotta—bright colored cloth, rolled in a circle, that women wear on their heads when carrying heavy baskets. Women are often seen wearing cottas and carrying bankra baskets full of vegetables or fruit on their way to market.

As you see, in Jamaica the languages and culture are a rich mixture of African, East Indian, Chinese, and European influences. Both English and Creole are spoken, and this is reflected in the "patois," or everyday speech of the people.

Enjoy!
Monica

Breadfruit

Captain Bligh brought
a treasure
many suns ago
to my island;
trees bearing fruit,
yellow-green and round,
we eat like bread.

We pick them each day
to boil or roast,
bake or fry.
And Grandma says,
"It's like manna sent,
thank God for trees
that give us bread."

The Merry-Go-Round

The music's begun. I'm excited it's here.
Once again in the village, we gather for fun.
My Grandma exclaims, "I'll ride a play mare!"
The music's begun.

The kerosene lanterns burn bright, there's no sun.
"All dem horses on poles, they come once a year.
Let's go chil'," she says spilling jars on the run
to gather the shillings she saved for the fare.
Together we ride, she's the frivolous one.
With laughter she bobs down, her eyes start to tear.
The music's begun.

Aunt Mae's Breadfruit Trees

"Chil', run down to Aunt Mae's yard
where breadfruit trees drooping with fruit.
Ask her to spare us one to eat,
want to cook me pepper pot soup."

Grandma's not ashamed to beg
when money's scarce like water in a drought.
Aunt Mae's fists never clench tight,
she often gives us two or three.

We have breadfruit to boil and roast
enough for breakfast, lunch, and dinner.
Grandma says, "God bless the poor man's bread,
and Aunt Mae's wide, open hands."

One Hand Washes the Other

Lean days try to hide
the sunshine from our lives
but Grandma won't let them.
She walks around the field,
picks a basket of callaloo leaves,
begs the butcher for a bone,
borrows a breadfruit from Aunt Mae
to make some callaloo soup.

Aunt Mae knows Grandma can sew
a dress for her little girl
faster than the hummingbird
sips nectar from a flower.
The butcher knows he'll get juicy canes
cut fresh from her field.
We feast on callaloo soup while Grandma winks,
"One hand washes the other."

Grandma and Aunt Jane

Grandma's only sister, Jane,
came to talk and laugh one day.
Like two congo peas in a pod,
didn't stay too long that way.

Grandma sighed, "How very sad!
Storm done blow poor Tom's house down."
Aunt Jane stamped, "Oh nonsense, Em!
It was a fire swept the town."

Raised their voices like the wind
getting louder with each gust.
The loving sisters hurled harsh words,
each one gave a deeper thrust.

They sat in church, two pious ones,
Parson preached, "Forgive, start new."
Grandma looked Jane in the eye,
"Did you hear? That was for you!"

The Leaky Gourd

"Go and fetch some water, girl!"
Grandma calls out loud today.
"Want to cook me callaloo,
don't you dally by the way."

Skipping down to Uncle's pond
I hum a tune in broiling sun.
Wading out, I fill my gourd
poke my toes in mud for fun.

Walking home, I feel the drips,
a leaky faucet down my back.
When Grandma takes the gourd, she scolds,
"Did I send you to wet de track?"

"Silly girl!" she says to me,
"Trek right back in scorching heat.
If you do not use your head,
take the blisters on your feet."

Tell the Truth

"Beauty is only skin deep,"
Grandma says to everyone.
Yet she laughs at my plain face,
brags my brother's is the sun.

Friends at school who tell white lies,
I tell them so with derring-do;
but dare not say to my Grandma,
"Why speak words that are not true?"

The Water Hose

I like to help Aunt Sue
spray water crystals from her hose
on drooping daisies.
I watch their faces brighten
into little smiling suns.

I like it better when I spray
those water crystals on myself;
feel them tickle and cool my skin,
brightening my face
into a smiling sun.

Bareback Riders

Getting ready to ride to the commons,
Grandpa and I don't bother with saddles.
Mounting on bareback is how we straddle,
holding our bridles to gallop away.

Biting its bit, mule's nervous and prancing.
Grandpa sits tall, he's a confident rider.
Flat on her back, I whisper to donkey,
"Giddyup girl! Come on, let's start trotting."

Grandpa rides fast, I'm trailing behind.
Chickens and goats scurry out of our way.
Breeze tickles my back, and donkey is braying.
Riding bareback, I'm bouncing and laughing.

Mean Old Aunt Aggie

Mean old Aunt Aggie,
sitting on the porch steps,
hawklike eyes keep watching
her ripe guavas falling.

My friend Connie and I know
to stay far from her fruit trees,
or we'll be stoned with curses
like the birds she chases.

Mean old Aunt Aggie,
never gives a fruit away.
May she slide on her pile
of rotting ripe guavas.

Russell Hill Neighbors

Uncle Ben raises pigs to sell.
The neighbors' scraps help make them fat.
Ready to kill the litter's best,
Russell Hill rallies with helping hands.

Fred and Uncle slay the squealing pig.
Sam singes hairs and scrapes its skin.
Nathan carves it into hocks and chops.
Mary cleans the long, ropelike tripe.

Cleveland gets the whole pig's head.
Mable cures the legs for ham.
Pork chops for Janie, Jim and Sam,
tripe for Mary who makes a feast.

No one's a stranger on Russell Hill.
Neighbors live like a close-knit clan.
Reaching out, they help each other.
Next month they'll share Nathan's goat.

When Grandpa Sells His Sugar Cane

When Grandpa sells his sugar cane,
we'll feast tonight.
Curry goat and rice,
corn pone topped with custard,
ice in our sorrel drink.
When Grandpa sells his sugar cane,
we'll feast tonight.

Uncle Viv

I watch the children passing by
staring through our latticed fence.
They walk around it once or twice
just to catch my uncle's eye.

"Hello, Mass Viv!" I hear them say,
with voices sweet as honey cakes;
yet their saddened faces plead,
"Can you spare a plum today?"

The children know my uncle well.
He stretches out his hands with plums
to every hungry face he sees;
gives away more than he leaves to sell.

"Why do you give so much?" I ask.
He says, "I too felt the hunger pain;
knew the joys of sharing hands.
I'll never break that giving chain."

Cousin Joe

Cousin Joe's facing real hard times.
White hair matted on his head,
smelly clothes are soiled and torn;
not even pennies line his pocket.

Often hungry inside his hut;
relatives shun him like stale fish.
Too weak to plant, old friends are gone;
only Mary thinks of him.

She leaves him a plate on her stove.
He goes to the kitchen, sits, and eats.
Smacking his lips, with a lively step,
he leaves there knowing someone cares.

High Tea

When Aunt Sue serves her fancy high tea,
we eat in the parlor on her settee.
Her crocheted doilies are pinned in place,
and tables so shiny to powder your face.
I feel real fancy and well-bred
eating sliced cucumber with bread.

At home my cornhusk doll and me
have our own afternoon high tea.
I sip pretend tea from a pink sea shell
that takes the place of a teacup well.
Eat Grandpa's cucumbers without the bread,
and still feel fancy and well bred.

Stella-Sue

Winding her way
to the Saturday market,
Stella-Sue walks
like a tall ballerina
balancing a fruit-filled
bankra basket
on her bright head cotta.

Oranges, bananas,
cashews, plums,
splashing sunshine colors
fill her basket
with ripe fruit scents;
enticing customers
to the Saturday market.

Hilda, the Higgler

Hilda's fancy sisters
look toward the skies
when they pass her
selling with the higglers.

"Not our class!" they whisper.
"Hear her call to tourists,
'Buy me spicy patties,
taste one, can't resist another.'"

If they only knew
with booming business,
Hilda needs octopus hands
to serve the lines that queue.

Christmas holidays are here.
Hilda flies to Miami.
Fancy sisters sit at home;
can't afford the fare.

Storyteller Nana

I think of Nana
sitting by the fireside,
cooking and humming calypso tunes;
me, on the hardened earth by her side.

"Tell me a story, Nana," I beg.
Her eyes light up like fireflies
and tales of Brer Anansi
flow from her lips.

When Nana tells her stories
it sounds as if she's reading.
No one would ever guess
she never learned to read a book.

Nana

Barefoot,
Nana walks the fields,
gathering dry sticks
to make her open fire.

She lights the small twigs,
stoops down, blows and blows . . .
like magic
her flames rise high.

Nana simmers congo peas
slow with rice;
makes the best corn pone
humming by her fire.

The Village Cobbler

Walking on rocky country roads
I hope to reach my school on time.
My loosened soles are flopping back.
Ashamed, I lag behind my friends.

I pass Mass Lester's cobbler shop;
it's on the road, along the way.
He knows to make old worn-out shoes
look like brand-new ones again.

With tear-filled eyes, I say to him,
"Please Mass Lester, tack my soles.
I cannot walk with floppy shoes,
stones poke my feet with every step."

He puts my shoes upon his last,
tacks the soles and hands them back.
Never charges for his time.
Thanking him, I skip to school.

Uncle Rufus

Uncle Rufus left our island shore,
sailed to Cuba seeking work.
Found a job, he saved and shopped,
came back home with fancy clothes.

On Sunday morning dressed for church,
he's a tail-spread peacock bird.
Eyes turn his way, left and right;
none can miss his gold tooth smile.

Jipijapa hat tilted on his head,
white suit pressed with ruler seams.
Collar starched and standing stiff,
gold watch dangling at his side.

Bulging bunions, twisted toes
poke through number fourteen shoes.
Uncle Rufus struts along—
handsome, but with peacock's feet.

My City Cousin

My city cousin comes to visit,
dressed in socks and patent leather,
fancy ribbons, fancy dress.
I squirm in old T-shirt and shorts.

My eyes can't leave her pretty clothes;
she looks at me, smiles, and shrugs.
"I hate these fancy things Ma buys,
wish I had your carefree clothes."

We shut the door and trade our clothes.
Giggles fill my tiny room.
She dashes off to play outside,
I stand frozen by the mirror.

I'm changed into the city cousin,
too dressed up, can't run and play.
Missing all the fun outside,
in fancy ribbons, fancy dress.

My Friend Connie

Connie and I are best of friends;
we play every day together.
Like our ackee and codfish dish,
never one without the other.

Running the three-legged race,
we sometimes topple in a pile.
Hobbling in last, it doesn't matter,
we grasp each other's hands and smile.

Connie whispers, "I have a treat.
I brought you two of Ma's bread ends."
We munch and tell each other jokes,
and vow we'll always be best friends.

Mangoes Are Ripening

No one goes hungry in our village,
mangoes are ripening.
I hear them dropping from the trees,
Bum! Bum! Bum!

Connie and I gather a pile.
We feast till our faces
turn yellow like the fruit.
No one goes hungry in our village,
mangoes are ripening.

Moonshine Dolly

My Jamaican moon beams brightly.
Connie and I place pebbles in a pile;
we'll play tonight, under the stars
our favorite game—Moonshine Dolly.

Connie lies down first, I lay pebbles
around her on the grass.
She makes my silhouette, like I did hers;
we're two dolls lying side by side.

We skip and giggle around those dolls
until Grandma's stern voice calls us in.
Our moonshine dollies linger like ghosts
glowing between the moonlight shadows.

Connie's Cake

Connie's coming over later;
been working hard on her surprise.
Saved two eggs from my red hen,
shook the buttermilk, made some butter.

I rubbed the butter and sugar well,
mixed in flour with milk and eggs.
Didn't forget nutmeg for spice,
set to bake in Grandma's Dutch oven.

When Connie came, I said to her,
"Happy birthday! Come see your surprise!"
Opened the Dutch oven, she burst out,
"You baked a bulla cake for me!"

I tried to smile, but cried instead.
"Connie! I forgot the baking powder!"
She hugs me tight, and winks her eye,
"Can't wait to taste my birthday bulla!"

The Waves

Waves rushing ashore
wash tears falling from my face
but the sadness stays
since Connie lays sick in bed
and I watch the waves alone.

The Wake

Two days ago when Connie died,
I cried, "No! No! this can't be true."
At her wake tonight, I can't deny
my best friend died; it's true.

People feast, they clap and sing,
a noisy way to say good-bye.
I tiptoe into Connie's room
to softly squeeze her hand good-bye.

I stare at her just lying there.
She's stiff and still, with lifeless hands.
Rush like the wind, far from her side,
afraid to touch my best friend's hands.

When Connie Died

When Connie died, I sat and cried.
Sadness lingered like a rainy day
whose steady dripping kept the chill inside.

At school, I didn't want to play.
No classmate there could take her place,
or be my partner for the race that May.

A new girl, Shirley, with a freckled face,
was someone many liked to tease.
She stood without a partner for the race.

I saw her face, which seemed so ill at ease,
I thought of Connie and knew what she would do.
Taking her hand, I gave a friendly squeeze.

She held my hand like Connie used to do.
I knew to Connie I was being true,
and Shirley's smile, my way of breaking through.

My Aunt Sue

Aunt Sue strokes
my face and hair
with hands worn rough
as dried cornhusks.

When she touches me
I'm a baby calf,
licked by a mother's tongue
soon after birth.

Her touch heals hurts,
calms my fears,
says, "Welcome to a world
where you'll find LOVE."

The Ravens

The ravens are back.
Coming together
in raucous company;
cawing and cawing
before the sun cracks the clouds.

The ravens are back,
outsquawking each other.
They chatter
like market women
hawking their cashew nuts.

Aunt Sara, the Gossip

Lawdy, Lawdy,
Look at Aunt Sara!
Hands talking fast
like her busy tongue.
She blabbers about,
"Did you hear?
Let me tell you—"

Lawdy, Lawdy,
don't heed Aunt Sara!
Telling her tales
spicy with lies.
Let her words die
like the flies we swat
to buzz no more.

Night Walk with Grandpa

We walk home at night
from the meeting hall,
moon and stars
our only lights.
Rocky stone roads
pinch my sandaled toes;
Grandpa and I
hurry along.

I stare at shadows
moving through the trees
like scary monsters
glaring down at me.
I shudder and cling
close to Grandpa,
feeling safe as we
hurry home.

My Parents

Papa and Mama left me
with Grandpa and Grandma
when I was only three.
I wonder, did they love me?

At Grandpa's side
I hear all the Bible stories.
We go for a donkey ride.
Grandpa loves me.

When I have my birthday,
Grandma sews me a new dress.
We picnic by the sea,
Grandma loves me.

Making Butter

Shaking the buttermilk for Grandma;
tiny mounds of butter float in my jar.
Looking up, I see passing cloud mountains
whisking by before my eyes.
Butter in the jar and clouds in the sky,
floating around like each other,
filling their own special spaces.

Ocean Breezes

Breezes
from the ocean
fanning my island's shores
lure rich and poor to swim in the
same seas.